For the men who fuelled my love of life on two wheels. — Kirli Saunders.

For Margaret Kennedy, who gives my creative machine freedom. — Matt Ottley.

Scholastic Canada Ltd.
604 King Street West, Toronto, Ontario M5V 1E1, Canada

Scholastic Inc.
557 Broadway, New York, NY 10012, USA

Scholastic Australia Pty Limited
PO Box 579, Gosford, NSW 2250, Australia

Scholastic New Zealand Limited
Private Bag 94407, Botany, Manukau 2163, New Zealand

Scholastic Children's Books
Euston House, 24 Eversholt Street, London NW1 1DB, UK

www.scholastic.ca

Typeset in Agent C.
Matt Ottley created the artwork in this book using oil paint on canvas.

Library and Archives Canada Cataloguing in Publication

Saunders, Kirli, author
The incredible freedom machines / Kirli Saunders
; [illustrated by] Matt Ottley.

Originally published: Lindfield, N.S.W.: Scholastic Australia, 2018.
ISBN 978-1-4431-7010-9 (hardcover).--ISBN 978-1-4431-7011-6
(softcover)

I. Ottley, Matt, illustrator II. Title.

PZ7.1.S28Inc 2019   j823'.92   C2018-906653-9

First published by Scholastic Australia in 2018.
This edition published by Scholastic Canada in 2019.

6 5 4 3 2 1   Printed in China 127   19 20 21 22 23 24

the
incredible
freed**o**m
machines

kirli saunders

matt ottley

Scholastic Canada Ltd.
Toronto New York London Auckland Sydney
Mexico City New Delhi Hong Kong Buenos Aires

She was small when she heard about them . . .

. . . the incredible freedom machines.

As she grew in a world sewn together by boundaries,

she saw the need
and hunted for one.

Freedom machines her size were hard to come by.

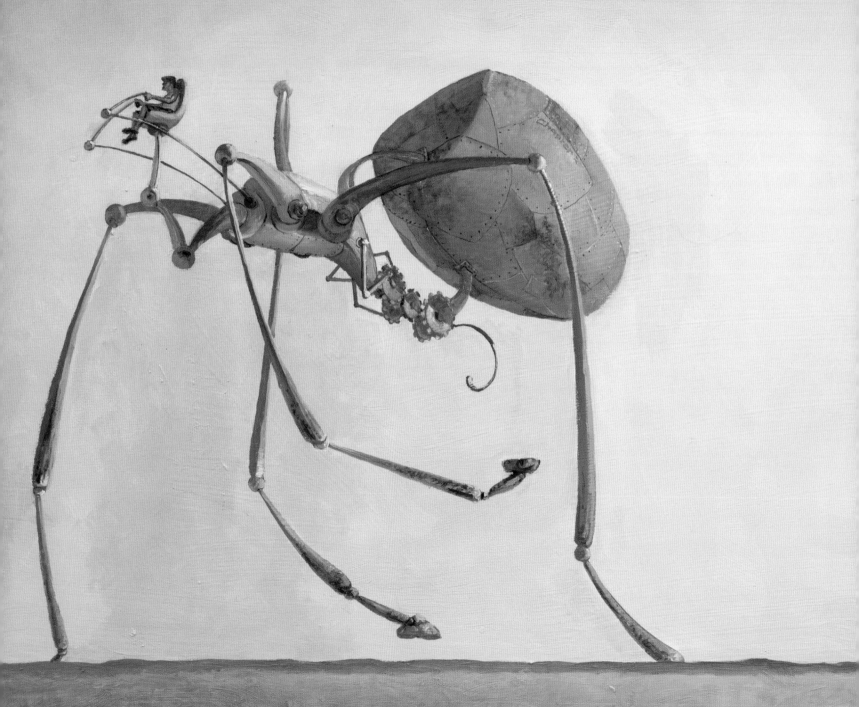

And the perfect one was toilsome to unearth.
It wasn't much, but it was hers.

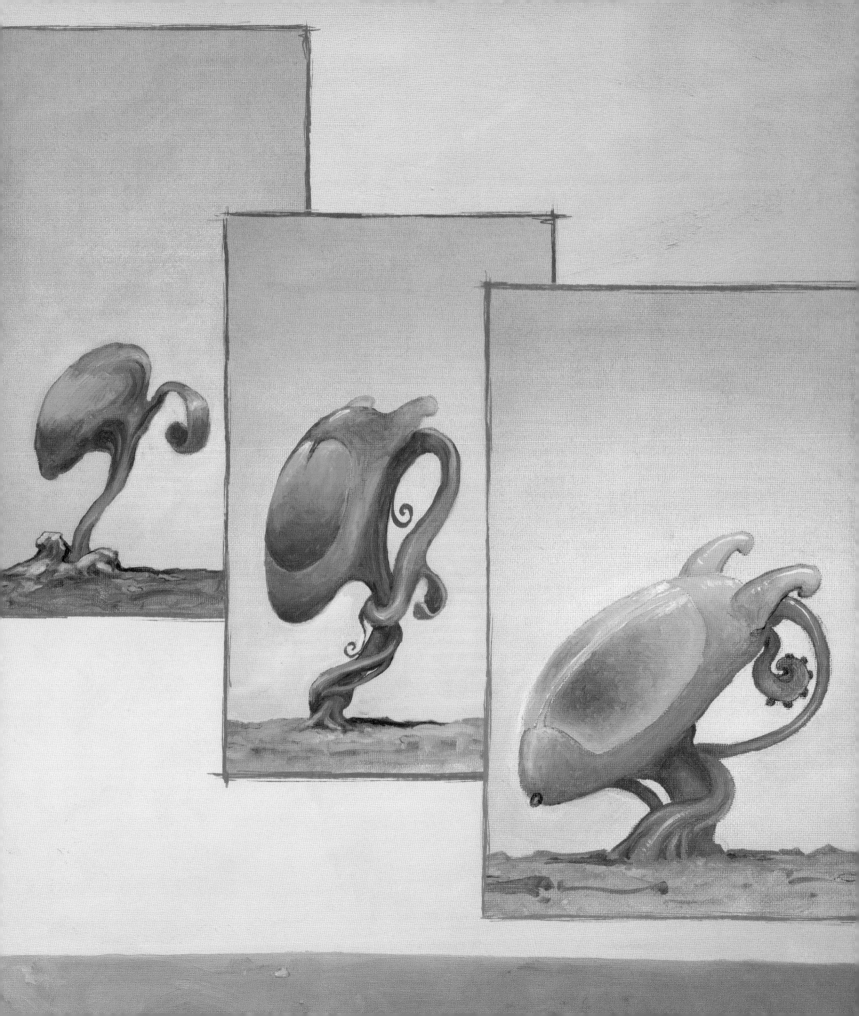

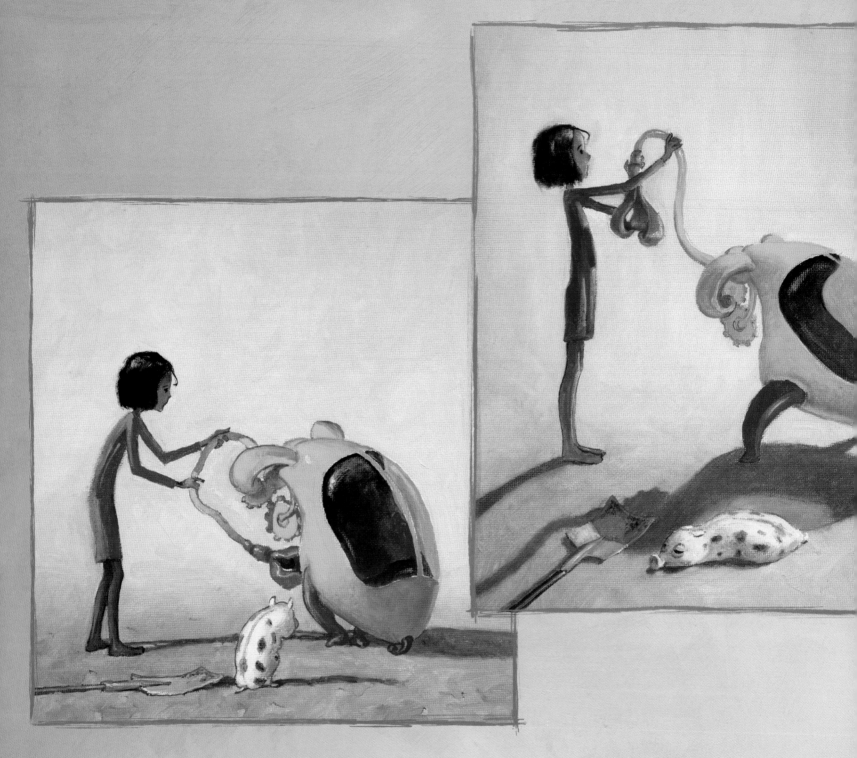

She adjusted the settings
and away she went.

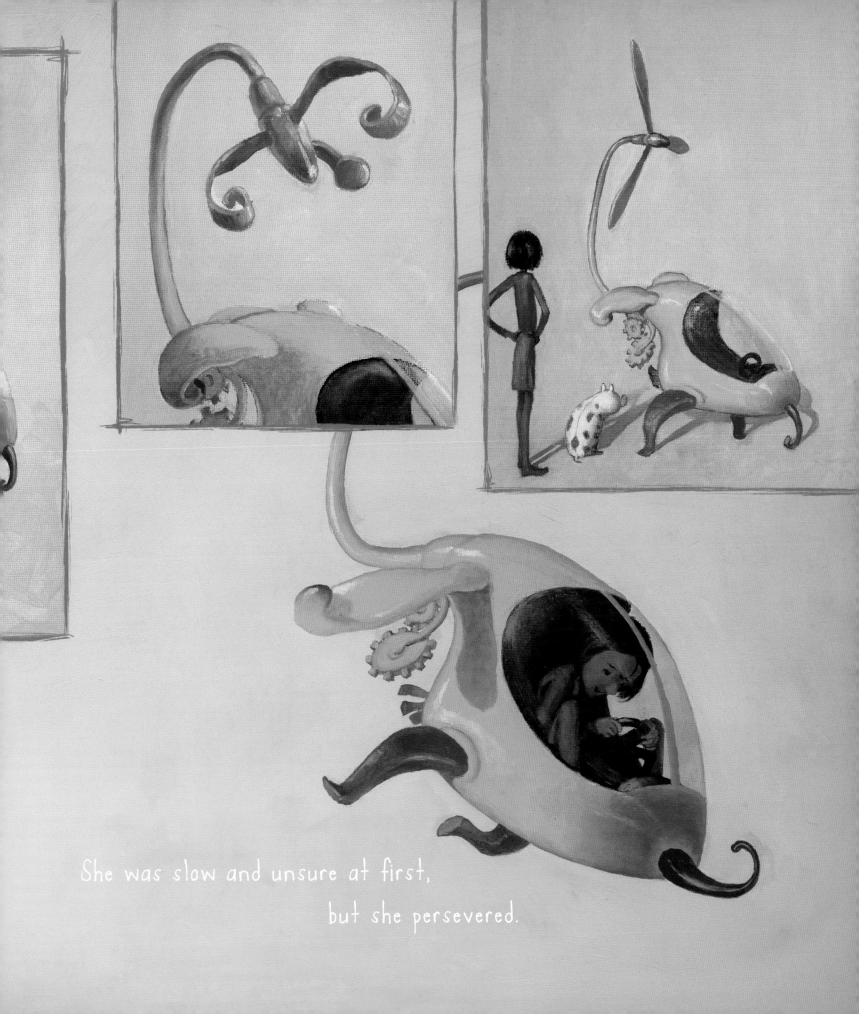

She was slow and unsure at first,
but she persevered.

Rainy days were no fun — the freedom machine leaked.
Windy days weren't much better.

But on the occasional day,
    when the weather was fine,
  everything would fall into place.

And on those days . . .

. . . she could fly.

Her freedom machine would take her
to the most lush, untouched places.

She would soak up their secrets
and return a little more entire.

With her freedom machine,
she was everything she had
ever dreamed of being.

In her unfurling world,
    it was all she would ever need.